MW01164661

A Reversible Santa Claus

Meredith Nicholson

In the interest of creating a more extensive selection of rare historical book reprints, we have chosen to reproduce this title even though it may possibly have occasional imperfections such as missing and blurred pages, missing text, poor pictures, markings, dark backgrounds and other reproduction issues beyond our control. Because this work is culturally important, we have made it available as a part of our commitment to protecting, preserving and promoting the world's literature. Thank you for your understanding.

A REVERSIBLE SANTA CLAUS

BY

MEREDITH NICHOLSON

WITH ILLUSTRATIONS BY

FLORENCE H. MINARD

BOSTON and NEW YORK
HOUGHTON MIFFLIN COMPANY
The Riverside Press, Cambridge
1917

COPYRIGHT, 1917, BY MEREDITH NICHOLSON

ALL RIGHTS RESERVED

Published October 1917

"DO YOU MIND TELLING ME JUST WHY YOU READ THAT
NOTE?" (*Page 78*)

Illustrations

From Drawings by F. Minard

2226889

A Reversible Santa Claus

I

A Reversible Santa Claus

I

MR. WILLIAM B. AIKINS, *alias* "Softy" Hubbard, *alias* Billy The Hopper, paused for breath behind a hedge that bordered a quiet lane and peered out into the highway at a roadster whose tail light advertised its presence to his felonious gaze. It was Christmas Eve, and after a day of unseasonable warmth a slow, drizzling rain was whimsically changing to snow.

The Hopper was blowing from two hours' hard travel over rough country. He

had stumbled through woodlands, flat-
tened himself in fence corners to avoid the
eyes of curious motorists speeding homeward or flying about distributing Christmas gifts, and he was now bent upon committing himself to an inter-urban trolley
line that would afford comfortable trans-
portation for the remainder of his journey.
Twenty miles, he estimated, still lay between him and his domicile.

The rain had penetrated his clothing
and vigorous exercise had not greatly di-
minished the chill in his blood. His heart
knocked violently against his ribs and he
was dismayed by his shortness of wind.
The Hopper was not so young as in the
days when his agility and genius for effect-
ing a quick "get-away" had earned for him
his sobriquet. The last time his Bertillon
measurements were checked (he was sub-

4

jected to this humiliating experience in Omaha during the Ak-Sar-Ben carnival three years earlier) official note was taken of the fact that The Hopper's hair, long carried in the records as black, was rapidly whitening.

At forty-eight a crook — even so resourceful and versatile a member of the fraternity as The Hopper — begins to mistrust himself. For the greater part of his life, when not in durance vile, The Hopper had been in hiding, and the state or condition of being a fugitive, hunted by keen-eyed agents of justice, is not, from all accounts, an enviable one. His latest experience of involuntary servitude had been under the auspices of the State of Oregon, for a trifling indiscretion in the way of safe-blowing. Having served his sentence, he skillfully effaced himself by

5

a year's siesta on a pine-apple plantation in Hawaii. The island climate was not wholly pleasing to The Hopper, and when pine-apples palled he took passage from Honolulu as a stoker, reached San Francisco (not greatly chastened in spirit), and by a series of characteristic hops, skips, and jumps across the continent landed in Maine by way of the Canadian provinces.

The Hopper needed money. He was not without a certain crude philosophy, and it had been his dream to acquire by some brilliant *coup* a sufficient fortune upon which to retire and live as a decent, law-abiding citizen for the remainder of his days. This ambition, or at least the means to its fulfillment, can hardly be defended as praiseworthy, but The Hopper was a singular character and we must take him as we find him. Many prison chaplains and jail visitors bearing tracts had striven with little success to implant moral ideals in the mind and soul of The Hopper, but he was still to be catalogued among the impenitent; and as he moved southward through the Commonwealth of Maine he was so oppressed by his poverty, as contrasted with the world's abundance, that he lifted forty thousand dollars in a neat bundle from an express car which Providence had sidetracked, apparently for his personal enrichment, on the upper waters of the Penobscot. Whereupon he began perforce playing his old game of artful dodging, exercising his best powers as a hopper and skipper. Forty thousand dollars is no inconsiderable sum of money, and the success of this master stroke of his career was not to be jeopardized by careless moves. By

craftily hiding in the big woods and making himself agreeable to isolated lumber-
jacks who rarely saw newspapers, he arrived in due course on Manhattan Island,
where with shrewd judgment he avoided
the haunts of his kind while planning a
future commensurate with his new dignity as a capitalist.

He spent a year as a diligent and faith-
ful employee of a garage which served
a fashionable quarter of the metropolis;
then, animated by a worthy desire to
continue to lead an honest life, he pur-
chased a chicken farm fifteen miles as
the crow flies from Center Church, New
Haven, and boldly opened a bank account in that academic center in his
newly adopted name of Charles S. Stevens, of Happy Hill Farm. Feeling the
need of companionship, he married a lady

somewhat his junior, a shoplifter of the second class, whom he had known before the vigilance of the metropolitan police necessitated his removal to the Far West. Mrs. Stevens's inferior talents as a petty larcenist had led her into many difficulties, and she gratefully availed herself of The Hopper's offer of his heart and hand.

They had added to their establishment a retired yegg who had lost an eye by the premature popping of the "soup" (i.e., nitro-glycerin) poured into the crevices of a country post-office in Missouri. In offering shelter to Mr. James Whitesides, *alias* "Humpy" Thompson, The Hopper's motives had not been wholly unselfish, as Humpy had been entrusted with the herding of poultry in several penitentiaries and was familiar with the most advanced scientific thought on chicken culture.

The roadster was headed toward his home and The Hopper contemplated it in the deepening dusk with greedy eyes. His labors in the New York garage had familiarized him with automobiles, and while he was not ignorant of the pains and penalties inflicted upon lawless persons who appropriate motors illegally, he was the victim of an irresistible temptation to jump into the machine thus left in the highway, drive as near home as he dared, and then abandon it. The owner of the roadster was presumably eating his evening meal in peace in the snug little cottage behind the shrubbery, and The Hopper was aware of no sound reason why he should not seize the vehicle and further widen the distance between him-

10

self and a suspicious-looking gentleman he had observed on the New Haven local.

The Hopper's conscience was not altogether at ease, as he had, that afternoon, possessed himself of a bill-book that was protruding from the breast-pocket of a dignified citizen whose strap he had shared in a crowded subway train. Having foresworn crime as a means of livelihood, The Hopper was chagrined that he had suffered himself to be beguiled into stealing by the mere propinquity of a piece of red leather. He was angry at the world as well as himself. People should not go about with bill-books sticking out of their pockets; it was unfair and unjust to those weak members of the human race who yield readily to temptation.

He had agreed with Mary when she married him and the chicken farm that they would respect the Ten Commandments and all statutory laws, State and Federal, and he was painfully conscious that when he confessed his sin she would deal severely with him. Even Humpy, now enjoying a peace that he had rarely known outside the walls of prison, even Humpy would be bitter. The thought that ne was again among the hunted would depress Mary and Humpy, and he knew that their harshness would be intensified because of his violation of the unwritten law of the underworld in resorting to purse-lifting, an infringement upon a branch of felony despicable and greatly inferior in dignity to safe-blowing.

These reflections spurred The Hopper to action, for the sooner he reached home the more quickly he could explain his protracted stay in New York (to which

metropolis he had repaired in the hope
of making a better price for eggs with
the commission merchants who handled
his products), submit himself to Mary's
chastisement, and promise to sin no more.
By returning on Christmas Eve, of all
times, again a fugitive, he knew that he
would merit the unsparing condemnation
that Mary and Humpy would visit upon
him. It was possible, it was even quite
likely, that the short, stocky gentleman
he had seen on the New Haven local was
not a "bull" — not really a detective
who had observed the little transaction
in the subway; but the very uncertainty
annoyed The Hopper. In his happy and
profitable year at Happy Hill Farm he
had learned to prize his personal comfort,
and he was humiliated to find that he had
been frightened into leaving the train at

Bansford to continue his journey afoot, and merely because a man had looked at him a little queerly.

Any Christmas spirit that had taken root in The Hopper's soul had been disturbed, not to say seriously threatened with extinction, by the untoward occurrences of the afternoon.

II

II

THE Hopper waited for a limousine to pass and then crawled out of his hiding-place, jumped into the roadster, and was at once in motion. He glanced back, fearing that the owner might have heard his departure, and then, satisfied of his immediate security, negotiated a difficult turn in the road and settled himself with a feeling of relief to careful but expeditious flight. It was at this moment, when he had urged the car to its highest speed, that a noise startled him — an amazing little chirrupy sound which corresponded to none of the familiar forewarnings of engine trouble. With his eyes to the front he listened for a repetition of the sound. It rose again — it was like a perplexing cheep and chirrup, changing to a chortle of glee.

"Goo-goo! Goo-goo-goo!"

The car was skimming a dark stretch of road and a superstitious awe fell upon The Hopper. Murder, he gratefully remembered, had never been among his crimes, though he had once winged a too-inquisitive policeman in Kansas City. He glanced over his shoulder, but saw no pursuing ghost in the snowy highway; then, looking down apprehensively, he detected on the seat beside him what appeared to be an animate bundle, and, prompted by a louder "goo-goo," he put out his hand. His fingers touched some-

18

thing warm and soft and were promptly seized and held by Something.

The Hopper snatched his hand free of the tentacles of the unknown and shook it violently. The nature of the Something troubled him. He renewed his experiments, steering with his left hand and exposing the right to what now seemed to be the grasp of two very small mittened hands.

"Goo-goo! Goody; teep wunnin'!"

"A kid!" The Hopper gasped.

That he had eloped with a child was the blackest of the day's calamities. He experienced a strange sinking feeling in the stomach. In moments of apprehension a crook's thoughts run naturally into periods of penal servitude, and the punishment for kidnaping, The Hopper recalled, was severe. He stopped the car and inspected his unwelcome fellow passenger by the light of matches. Two big blue eyes stared at him from a hood and two mittens were poked into his face. Two small feet, wrapped tightly in a blanket, kicked at him energetically.

"Detup! Mate um skedaddle!"

Obedient to this command The Hopper made the car skedaddle, but superstitious dread settled upon him more heavily. He was satisfied now that from the moment he transferred the strap-hanger's bill-book to his own pocket he had been hoodooed. Only a jinx of the most malevolent type could have prompted his hurried exit from a train to dodge an imaginary "bull." Only the blackest of evil spirits could be responsible for this involuntary kidnaping!

"Mate um wun! Mate um 'ippity stip!"

A Reversible Santa Claus

The mittened hands reached for the wheel at this juncture and an unlooked-for "jippity skip" precipitated the young passenger into The Hopper's lap.

This mishap was attended with the jolliest baby laughter. Gently but with much firmness The Hopper restored the youngster to an upright position and supported him until sure he was able to sustain himself.

"Ye better set still, little feller," he admonished.

The little feller seemed in no wise astonished to find himself abroad with a perfect stranger and his courage and good cheer were not lost upon The Hopper. He wanted to be severe, to vent his rage for the day's calamities upon the only human being within range, but in spite of himself he felt no animosity toward the

friendly little bundle of humanity beside
him. Still, he had stolen a baby and it was
incumbent upon him to free himself at
once of the appalling burden; but a baby
is not so easily disposed of. He could not,
without seriously imperiling his liberty,
return to the cottage. It was the rule of
house-breakers, he recalled, to avoid babies. He had heard it said by burglars
of wide experience and unquestioned wis-
dom that babies were the most dangerous of all burglar alarms. All things con-
sidered, kidnaping and automobile theft
were not a happy combination with which
to appear before a criminal court. The
Hopper was vexed because the child did
not cry; if he had shown a bad disposition The Hopper might have abandoned
him; but the youngster was the cheeriest
and most agreeable of traveling compan-

ions. Indeed, The Hopper's spirits rose under his continued "goo-gooing" and chirruping.

"Nice little Shaver!" he said, patting the child's knees.

Little Shaver was so pleased by this friendly demonstration that he threw up his arms in an effort to embrace The Hopper.

"Bil-lee," he gurgled delightedly.

The Hopper was so astonished at being addressed in his own lawful name by a strange baby that he barely averted a collision with a passing motor truck. It was unbelievable that the baby really knew his name, but perhaps it was a good omen that he had hit upon it. The Hopper's resentment against the dark fate that seemed to pursue him vanished. Even though he had stolen a baby, it was

23

a merry, brave little baby who did n't
mind at all being run away with! He dismissed the thought of planting the little
shaver at a door, ringing the bell and
running away; this was no way to treat a
friendly child that had done him no in-
jury, and The Hopper highly resolved to
do the square thing by the youngster even
at personal inconvenience and risk.

The snow was now falling in generous
Christmasy flakes, and the high speed
the car had again attained was evidently
deeply gratifying to the young person,
whose reckless tumbling about made it
necessary for The Hopper to keep a hand
on him.

"Steady, little un; steady!" The Hopper kept mumbling.

His wits were busy trying to devise
some means of getting rid of the young-

ster without exposing himself to the danger of arrest. By this time some one was
undoubtedly busily engaged in searching
for both baby and car; the police far and
near would be notified, and would be on
the lookout for a smart roadster containing a stolen child.

"Merry Christmas!" a boy shouted
from a farm gate.

"M'y Kwismus!" piped Shaver.

The Hopper decided to run the machine
home and there ponder the disposition
of his blithe companion with the care the
unusual circumstances demanded.

"'Urry up; me's goin' 'ome to me's
gwanpa's kwismus t'ee!"

"Right ye be, little un; right ye be!"
affirmed The Hopper.

The youngster was evidently blessed
with a sanguine and confiding nature.

25

His reference to his grandfather's Christmas tree impinged sharply upon The Hopper's conscience. Christmas had never figured very prominently in his scheme of life. About the only Christmases that he recalled with any pleasure were those that he had spent in prison, and those were marked only by Christmas dinners varying with the generosity of a series of wardens.

But Shaver was entitled to all the joys of Christmas, and The Hopper had no desire to deprive him of them.

"Keep a-larfin', Shaver, keep a-larfin'," said the Hopper. "Ole Hop ain't a-goin' to hurt ye!"

The Hopper, feeling his way cautiously round the fringes of New Haven, arrived presently at Happy Hill Farm, where he ran the car in among the chicken sheds

behind the cottage and carefully extin-
guished the lights.

"Now, Shaver, out ye come!"

Whereupon Shaver obediently jumped
into his arms.

III

III

THE Hopper knocked twice at the back
door, waited an instant, and knocked
again. As he completed the signal the
door was opened guardedly. A man and
woman surveyed him in hostile silence
as he pushed past them, kicked the
door shut, and deposited the blinking
child on the kitchen table. Humpy, the
one-eyed, jumped to the windows and
jammed the green shades close into the
frames. The woman scowlingly waited
for the head of the house to explain himself, and this, with the perversity of one

31

who knows the dramatic value of suspense, he was in no haste to do.

"Well," Mary questioned sharply. "What ye got there, Bill?"

The Hopper was regarding Shaver with a grin of benevolent satisfaction. The youngster had seized a bottle of catsup and was making heroic efforts to raise it to his mouth, and the Hopper was intensely tickled by Shaver's efforts to swallow the bottle. Mrs. Stevens, *alias* Weeping Mary, was not amused, and her husband's enjoyment of the child's antics irritated her.

"Come out with ut, Bill!" she commanded, seizing the bottle. "What ye been doin'?"

Shaver's big blue eyes expressed surprise and displeasure at being deprived of his plaything, but he recovered quickly

32

and reached for a plate with which he began thumping the table.

"Out with ut, Hop!" snapped Humpy nervously. "Nothin' wuz said about kidnapin', an' I don't stand for ut!"

"When I heard the machine comin' in the yard I knowed somethin' was wrong an' I guess it could n't be no worse," added Mary, beginning to cry. "You had n't no right to do ut, Bill. Hookin' a buzz-buzz an' a kid an' when we wuz playin' the white card! You ought t' 'a' told me, Bill, what ye went to town fer, an' it bein' Christmas, an' all."

That he should have chosen for his fall the Christmas season of all times was reprehensible, a fact which Mary and Humpy impressed upon him in the strongest terms. The Hopper was fully aware of the inopportuneness of his transgressions,

but not to the point of encouraging his
wife to abuse him.

As he clumsily tried to unfasten Shaver's hood, Mary pushed him aside and
with shaking fingers removed the child's
wraps. Shaver's cheeks were rosy from
his drive through the cold; he was a
plump, healthy little shaver and The
Hopper viewed him with intense pride.
Mary held the hood and coat to the light
and inspected them with a sophisticated
eye. They were of excellent quality and
workmanship, and she shook her head
and sighed deeply as she placed them
carefully on a chair.

"It ain't on the square, Hop," protested
Humpy, whose lone eye expressed the
most poignant sorrow at The Hopper's
derelictions. Humpy was tall and lean,
with a thin, many-lined face. He was an

ill-favored person at best, and his habit
of turning his head constantly as though
to compel his single eye to perform double
service gave one an impression of restless
watchfulness.

"Cute little Shaver, ain't 'e? Give
Shaver somethin' to eat, Mary. I guess
milk'll be the right ticket considerin' th'
size of 'im. How ole you make 'im? Not
more'n three, I reckon?"

"Two. He ain't more'n two, that kid."

"A nice little feller; you're a cute un,
ain't ye, Shaver?"

Shaver nodded his head solemnly.
Having wearied of playing with the plate
he gravely inspected the trio; found something amusing in Humpy's bizarre coun-
tenance and laughed merrily. Finding no
response to his friendly overtures he ap-
pealed to Mary.

"Me wants me's paw-widge," he announced.

"Porridge," interpreted Humpy with the air of one whose superior breeding makes him the proper arbiter of the speech of children of high social station. Whereupon Shaver appreciatively poked his forefinger into Humpy's surviving optic.

"I'll see what I got," muttered Mary. "What ye used t' eatin' for supper, honey?"

The "honey" was a concession, and The Hopper, who was giving Shaver his watch to play with, bent a commendatory glance upon his spouse.

"Go on an' tell us what ye done," said Mary, doggedly busying herself about the stove.

The Hopper drew a chair to the table

to be within reach of Shaver and related succinctly his day's adventures.

"A dip!" moaned Mary as he described the seizure of the purse in the subway.

"You had n't no right to do ut, Hop!" bleated Humpy, who had tipped his chair against the wall and was sucking a cold pipe. And then, professional curiosity overmastering his shocked conscience, he added: "What'd she measure, Hop?"

The Hopper grinned.

"Flubbed! Nothin' but papers," he confessed ruefully.

Mary and Humpy expressed their indignation and contempt in unequivocal terms, which they repeated after he told of the suspected "bull" whose presence on the local had so alarmed him. A frank description of his flight and of his seizure

37

of the roadster only added to their bitter-
ness.

Humpy rose and paced the floor with
the quick, short stride of men habituated
to narrow spaces. The Hopper watched
the telltale step so disagreeably reminis-
cent of evil times and shrugged his shoulders impatiently.

"Set down, Hump; ye make me nervous. I got thinkin' to do."

"Ye'd better be quick about doin' ut!"
Humpy snorted with an oath.

"Cut the cussin'!" The Hopper admonished sharply. Since his retirement to
private life he had sought diligently to
free his speech of profanity and thieves'
slang, as not only unbecoming in a re-
spectable chicken farmer, but likely to
arouse suspicions as to his origin and
previous condition of servitude. "Can't

38

ye see Shaver ain't use to ut? Shaver's a little gent; he's a reg'ler little juke; that's wot Shaver is."

"The more 'way up he is the worse fer us," whimpered Humpy. "It's kidnapin', that's wot ut is!"

"That's wot it *ain't*," declared The Hopper, averting a calamity to his watch, which Shaver was swinging by its chain. "He was took by accident I tell ye! I'm goin' to take Shaver back to his ma — ain't I, Shaver?"

"Take 'im back!" echoed Mary.

Humpy crumpled up in his chair at this new evidence of The Hopper's insanity.

"I'm goin' to make a Chris'mas present o' Shaver to his ma," reaffirmed The Hopper, pinching the nearer ruddy cheek of the merry, contented guest.

A Reversible Santa Claus

Shaver kicked The Hopper in the stomach and emitted a chortle expressive of unshakable confidence in The Hopper's ability to restore him to his lawful owners. This confidence was not, however, manifested toward Mary, who had prepared with care the only cereal her pantry afforded, and now approached Shaver, bowl and spoon in hand. Shaver, taken by surprise, inspected his supper with disdain and spurned it with a vigor that sent the spoon rattling across the floor.

"Me wants me's paw-widge bowl! Me wants me's *own* paw-widge bowl!" he screamed.

Mary expostulated; Humpy offered advice as to the best manner of dealing with the refractory Shaver, who gave further expression to his resentment by throwing The Hopper's watch with vio-

lence against the wall. That the table-
service of The Hopper's establishment
was not to Shaver's liking was manifested
in repeated rejections of the plain white
bowl in which Mary offered the porridge.
He demanded his very own porridge bowl
with the increasing vehemence of one who
is willing to starve rather than accept so
palpable a substitute. He threw himself
back on the table and lay there kicking
and crying. Other needs now occurred to
Shaver: he wanted his papa; he wanted
his mamma; he wanted to go to his
gwan'pa's. He clamored for Santa Claus
and numerous Christmas trees which, it
seemed, had been promised him at the
houses of his kinsfolk. It was amazing
and bewildering that the heart of one so
young could desire so many things that
were not immediately attainable. He had

begun to suspect that he was among
strangers who were not of his way of life,
and this was fraught with the gravest
danger.

"They'll hear 'im hollerin' in China,"
wailed the pessimistic Humpy, running
about the room and examining the fast-
enings of doors and windows. "Folks
goin' along the road'll hear 'im, an' it's
terms fer the whole bunch!"

The Hopper began pacing the floor
with Shaver, while Humpy and Mary de-
nounced the child for unreasonableness
and lack of discipline, not overlooking the
stupidity and criminal carelessness of The
Hopper in projecting so lawless a youngster into their domestic circle.

"Twenty years, that's wot ut is!"
mourned Humpy.

"Ye kin get the chair fer kidnapin',"

A Reversible Santa Claus

Mary added dolefully. "Ye gotta get 'im out o' here, Bill."

Pleasant predictions of a long prison term with capital punishment as the happy alternative failed to disturb The Hopper. To their surprise and somewhat to their shame he won the Shaver to a tractable humor. There was nothing in The Hopper's known past to justify any expectation that he could quiet a crying baby, and yet Shaver with a child's unerring instinct realized that The Hopper meant to be kind. He patted The Hopper's face with one fat little paw, chokingly declaring that he was hungry.

"'Course Shaver's hungry; an' Shaver's goin' to eat nice porridge Aunt Mary made fer 'im. Shaver's goin' to have 'is own porridge bowl to-morry — yes, sir-ee, oo is, little Shaver!"

Restored to the table, Shaver opened his mouth in obedience to The Hopper's patient pleading and swallowed a spoonful of the mush, Humpy holding the bowl out of sight in tactful deference to the child's delicate æsthetic sensibilities. A tumbler of milk was sipped with grateful gasps.

The Hopper grinned, proud of his success, while Mary and Humpy viewed his efforts with somewhat grudging admiration, and waited patiently until The Hopper took the wholly surfeited Shaver in his arms and began pacing the floor, humming softly. In normal circumstances The Hopper was not musical, and Humpy and Mary exchanged looks which, when interpreted, pointed to nothing less than a belief that the owner of Happy Hill Farm was bereft of his senses. There was some question as

44

THE HOPPER GRINNED, PROUD OF HIS SUCCESS, WHICH MARY
AND HUMPY VIEWED WITH GRUDGING ADMIRATION

to whether Shaver should be undressed. Mary discouraged the idea and Humpy took a like view.

"Ye gotta chuck 'im quick; that's what ye gotta do," said Mary hoarsely. "We don't want 'im sleepin' here."

Whereupon The Hopper demonstrated his entire independence by carrying the Shaver to Humpy's bed and partially undressing him. While this was in progress, Shaver suddenly opened his eyes wide and raising one foot until it approximated the perpendicular, reached for it with his chubby hands.

"Sant' Claus comin'; m'y Kwismus!"

"Jes' listen to Shaver!" chuckled The Hopper. "''Course Santy is comin,' an' we're goin' to hang up Shaver's stockin', ain't we, Shaver?"

He pinned both stockings to the foot-

board of Humpy's bed. By the time this
was accomplished under the hostile eyes
of Mary and Humpy, Shaver slept the
sleep of the innocent.

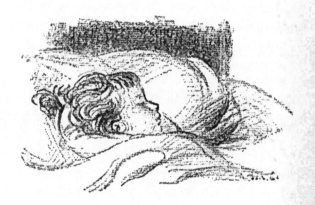

IV

IV

THEY watched the child in silence for a few minutes and then Mary detached a gold locket from his neck and bore it to the kitchen for examination.

"Ye gotta move quick, Hop," Humpy urged. "The white card's what we wuz all goin' to play. We wuz fixed nice here, an' things goin' easy; an' the yard full o' br'ilers. I don't want to do no more time. I'm an ole man, Hop."

"Cut ut!" ordered The Hopper, taking the locket from Mary and weighing it critically in his hand. They bent over him

as he scrutinized the face on which was
inscribed: —

Roger Livingston Talbot

June 13, 1913

"Lemme see; he's two an' a harf. Ye
purty nigh guessed 'im right, Mary."

The sight of the gold trinket, the proba-
bility that the Shaver belonged to a family of wealth, proved disturbing to Humpy's late protestations of virtue.

"They'd be a heap o' kale in ut, Hop.
His folks is rich, I reckon. Ef we wuz n't
playin' the white card —"

Ignoring this shocking evidence of
Humpy's moral instability, The Hopper
became lost in reverie, meditatively drawing at his pipe.

"We ain't never goin' to quit playin' ut
square," he announced, to Mary's mani-

fest relief. "I had n't ought t' 'a' done th'
dippin'. It were a mistake. My ole head
wuz n't workin' right er I would n't 'a'
slipped. But ye need n't jump on me no
more."

"Wot ye goin' to do with that kid? Ye
tell me that!" demanded Mary, unwilling
too readily to accept The Hopper's re-
pentance at face value.

"I'm goin' to take 'im to 'is folks,
that's wot I'm goin' to do with 'im," announced The Hopper.

"Yer crazy — yer plum' crazy!" cried
Humpy, slapping his knees excitedly.
"Ye kin take 'im to an orphant asylum
an' tell um ye found 'im in that machine
ye lifted. And mebbe ye'll git by with ut
an' mebbe ye won't, but ye gotta keep
me out of ut!"

"I found the machine in th' road, right

here by th' house; an' th' kid was in ut all
by hisself. An' bein' humin an' respecti-
ble I brought 'im in to keep 'im from
freezin' t' death," said The Hopper, as
though repeating lines he was committing
to memory. "They ain't nobody can say
as I did n't. Ef I git pinched, that's my
spiel to th' cops. It ain't kidnapin'; it's
life-savin', that's wot ut is! I'm a-goin'
back an' have a look at that place where
I got 'im. Kind o' queer they left the
kid out there in the buzz-wagon; *mighty*
queer, now's I think of ut. Little house
back from the road; lots o' trees an'
bushes in front. Did n't seem to be no
lights. He keeps talkin' about Chris'mas
at his grandpa's. Folks must 'a' been
goin' to take th' kid somewheres fer
Chris'mas. I guess it'll throw a skeer into
'em to find him up an' gone."

A Reversible Santa Claus

"They's rich, an' all the big bulls 'll be lookin' fer 'im; ye'd better 'phone the New Haven cops ye've picked 'im up. Then they 'll come out, an' yer spiel about findin' 'im 'll sound easy an' sensible like."

The Hopper, puffing his pipe philosophically, paid no heed to Humpy's suggestion even when supported warmly by Mary.

"I gotta find some way o' puttin' th' kid back without seein' no cops. I 'll jes' take a sneak back an' have a look at th' place," said The Hopper. "I ain't goin' to turn Shaver over to no cops. Ye can't take no chances with 'em. They don't know nothin' about us bein' here, but they ain't fools, an' I ain't goin' to give none o' 'em a squint at me!"

He defended his plan against a joint attack by Mary and Humpy, who saw in

it only further proof of his tottering reason. He was obliged to tell them in harsh
terms to be quiet, and he added to their
rage by the deliberation with which he
made his preparations to leave.

He opened the door of a clock and drew
out a revolver which he examined carefully and thrust into his pocket. Mary
groaned; Humpy beat the air in impotent
despair. The Hopper possessed himself
also of a jimmy and an electric lamp.
The latter he flashed upon the face of the
sleeping Shaver, who turned restlessly for
a moment and then lay still again. He
smoothed the coverlet over the tiny form,
while Mary and Humpy huddled in the
doorway. Mary wept; Humpy was awed
into silence by his old friend's perversity.
For years he had admired The Hopper's
cleverness, his genius for extricating him-

self from difficulties; he was deeply shaken
to think that one who had stood so high
in one of the most exacting of professions
should have fallen so low. As The Hopper imperturbably buttoned his coat and
walked toward the door, Humpy set his
back against it in a last attempt to save
his friend from his own foolhardiness.

"Ef anybody turns up here an' asks
for th' kid, ye kin tell 'em wot I said. We
finds 'im in th' road right here by the
farm when we're doin' th' night chores
an' takes 'im in t' keep 'im from freezin'.
Ye'll have th' machine an' kid here to
show 'em. An' as fer me, I'm off lookin'
fer his folks."

Mary buried her face in her apron and
wept despairingly. The Hopper, noting
for the first time that Humpy was guard-
ing the door, roughly pushed him aside

and stood for a moment with his hand on the knob.

"They's things wot is," he remarked with a last attempt to justify his course, "an' things wot ain't. I reckon I'll take a peek at that place an' see wot's th' best way t' shake th' kid. Ye can't jes' run up to a house in a machine with his folks all settin' round cryin' an' cops askin' questions. Ye got to do some plannin' an' thinkin'. I'm goin' t' clean ut all up before daylight, an' ye need n't worry none about ut. Hop ain't worryin'; jes' leave ut t' Hop!"

There was no alternative but to leave it to Hop, and they stood mute as he went out and softly closed the door.

V

V

THE snow had ceased and the stars shone brightly on a white world as The Hopper made his way by various trolley lines to the house from which he had snatched Shaver. On a New Haven car he debated the prospects of more snow with a policeman who seemed oblivious to the fact that a child had been stolen — shamelessly carried off by a man with a long police record. Merry Christmas passed from lip to lip as if all creation were attuned to the note of love and peace, and crime were an undreamed-of thing.

A Reversible Santa Claus

For two years The Hopper had led an exemplary life and he was keenly alive now to the joy of adventure. His lapses of the day were unfortunate; he thought of them with regret and misgivings, but he was zestful for whatever the unknown held in store for him. Abroad again with a pistol in his pocket, he was a lawless being, but with the difference that he was intent now upon making restitution, though in such manner as would give him something akin to the old thrill that he experienced when he enjoyed the reputation of being one of the most skillful yeggs in the country. The successful thief is of necessity an imaginative person; he must be able to visualize the unseen and to deal with a thousand hidden contingencies. At best the chances are against him; with all his ingenuity the broad, heavy hand of the law is likely at any moment to close upon him from some unexpected quarter. The Hopper knew this, and knew, too, that in yielding to the exhilaration of the hour he was likely to come to grief. Justice has a long memory, and if he again made himself the object of police scrutiny that little forty-thousand-dollar affair in Maine might still be fixed upon him.

When he reached the house from whose gate he had removed the roadster with Shaver attached, he studied it with the eye of an experienced strategist. No gleam anywhere published the presence of frantic parents bewailing the loss of a baby. The cottage lay snugly behind its barrier of elms and shrubbery as though its young heir had not vanished into the void. The Hopper was a deliberating be-

ing and he gave careful weight to these
circumstances as he crept round the
walk, in which the snow lay undisturbed,
and investigated the rear of the premises.
The lattice door of the summer kitchen
opened readily, and, after satisfying
himself that no one was stirring in the
lower part of the house, he pried up the
sash of a window and stepped in. The
larder was well stocked, as though in
preparation for a Christmas feast, and he
passed on to the dining-room, whose ap-
pointments spoke for good taste and a
degree of prosperity in the householder.

Cautious flashes of his lamp disclosed
on the table a hamper, in which were
packed a silver cup, plate, and bowl which
at once awoke the Hopper's interest.
Here indubitably was proof that this was
the home of Shaver, now sleeping sweetly

in Humpy's bed, and this was the porridge
bowl for which Shaver's soul had yearned.
If Shaver did not belong to the house, he
had at least been a visitor there, and it
struck The Hopper as a reasonable as-
sumption that Shaver had been deposited
in the roadster while his lawful guardians
returned to the cottage for the hamper
preparatory to an excursion of some sort.
But The Hopper groped in the dark for an
explanation of the calmness with which
the householders accepted the loss of the
child. It was not in human nature for the
parents of a youngster so handsome and
in every way so delightful as Shaver to
permit him to be stolen from under their
very noses without making an outcry.
The Hopper examined the silver pieces
and found them engraved with the
name borne by the locket. He crept

through a living-room and came to a Christmas tree — the smallest of Christmas trees. Beside it lay a number of packages designed clearly for none other than young Roger Livingston Talbot.

Housebreaking is a very different business from the forcible entry of country post-offices, and The Hopper was nervous. This particular house seemed utterly deserted. He stole upstairs and found doors open and a disorder indicative of the occupants' hasty departure. His attention was arrested by a small room finished in white, with a white enameled bed, and other furniture to match. A generous litter of toys was the last proof needed to establish the house as Shaver's true domicile. Indeed, there was every indication that Shaver was the central figure of this home of whose

charm and atmosphere The Hopper was
vaguely sensible. A frieze of dancing children and water-color sketches of Shaver's
head, dabbed here and there in the most
unlooked-for places, hinted at an artistic
household. This impression was strength-
ened when The Hopper, bewildered and
baffled, returned to the lower floor and
found a studio opening off the living-
room. The Hopper had never visited a
studio before, and, satisfied now that he
was the sole occupant of the house, he
passed about shooting his light upon un-
finished canvases, pausing finally before
an easel supporting a portrait of Shaver
— newly finished, he discovered, by pok-
ing his finger into the wet paint. Something fell to the floor and he picked up
a large sheet of drawing-paper on which
this message was written in charcoal: —

A Reversible Santa Claus

Six-thirty.

Dear Sweetheart: —

This is a fine trick you have played on me, you dear girl! I've been expecting you back all afternoon. At six I decided that you were going to spend the night with your infuriated parent and thought I'd try my luck with mine! I put Billie into the roadster and, leaving him there, ran over to the Flemings's to say Merry Christmas and tell 'em we were off for the night. They kept me just a minute to look at those new Jap prints Jim's so crazy about, and while I was gone you came along and skipped with Billie and the car! I suppose this means that you've been making headway with your dad and want to try the effect of Billie's blandishments. Good luck! But you might have stopped long enough to tell me about it! How fine it would be if everything could be straightened out for Christmas! Do you remember the first time I kissed you — it was on Christmas Eve four years ago at the Billings's dance! I'm just trolleying out to father's to see what an evening session will do. I'll be back early in the morning.

Love always,

ROGER.

66

A Reversible Santa Claus

Billie was undoubtedly Shaver's nick-
name. This delighted The Hopper. That
they should possess the same name appeared to create a strong bond of com-
radeship. The writer of the note was presumably the child's father and the "Dear
Sweetheart" the youngster's mother. The
Hopper was not reassured by these disclos-
ures. The return of Shaver to his parents
was far from being the pleasant little
Christmas Eve adventure he had imag-
ined. He had only the lowest opinion of a
father who would, on a winter evening,
carelessly leave his baby in a motor-car
while he looked at pictures, and who, finding both motor and baby gone, would
take it for granted that the baby's
mother had run off with them. But these
people were artists, and artists, The Hopper had heard, were a queer breed, sadly

67

lacking in common sense. He tore the note into strips which he stuffed into his pocket.

Depressed by the impenetrable wall of mystery along which he was groping, he returned to the living-room, raised one of the windows and unbolted the front door to make sure of an exit in case these strange, foolish Talbots should unexpectedly return. The shades were up and he shielded his light carefully with his cap as he passed rapidly about the room. It began to look very much as though Shaver would spend Christmas at Happy Hill Farm—a possibility that had not figured in The Hopper's calculations.

Flashing his lamp for a last survey a letter propped against a lamp on the table arrested his eye. He dropped to the floor and crawled into a corner where he turned his light upon the note and read, not without difficulty, the following: —

Seven o'clock.

Dear Roger: —

I've just got back from father's where I spent the last three hours talking over our troubles. I did n't tell you I was going, knowing you would think it foolish, but it seemed best, dear, and I hope you'll forgive me. And now I find that you've gone off with Billie, and I'm guessing that you've gone to *your* father's to see what you can do. I'm taking the trolley into New Haven to ask Mamie Palmer about that cook she thought we might get, and if possible I'll bring the girl home with me. Don't trouble about me, as I'll be perfectly safe, and, as you know, I rather enjoy prowling around at night. You'll certainly get back before I do, but if I'm not here don't be alarmed.

We are so happy in each other, dear, and if only we could get our foolish fathers to stop hating each other, how beautiful everything would be! And we could all have such a merry, merry Christmas!

MURIEL.

A Reversible Santa Claus

The Hopper's acquaintance with the epistolary art was the slightest, but even to a mind unfamiliar with this branch of literature it was plain that Shaver's parents were involved in some difficulty that was attributable, not to any lessening of affection between them, but to a row of some sort between their respective fathers. Muriel, running into the house to write her note, had failed to see Roger's letter in the studio, and this was very fortunate for The Hopper; but Muriel might return at any moment, and it would add nothing to the plausibility of the story he meant to tell if he were found in the house.

VI

VI

ANXIOUS and dejected at the increasing difficulties that confronted him, he was moving toward the door when a light, buoyant step sounded on the veranda. In a moment the living-room lights were switched on from the entry and a woman called out sharply: —

"Stop right where you are or I'll shoot!"

The authoritative voice of the speaker, the quickness with which she had grasped the situation and leveled her revolver, brought The Hopper to an abrupt halt in

73

the middle of the room, where he fell with
a discordant crash across the keyboard of
a grand piano. He turned, cowering, to
confront a tall, young woman in a long
ulster who advanced toward him slowly,
but with every mark of determination
upon her face. The Hopper stared beyond
the gun, held in a very steady hand, into
a pair of fearless dark eyes. In all his ex-
periences he had never been cornered by a
woman, and he stood gaping at his captor
in astonishment. She was a very pretty
young woman, with cheeks that still had
the curve of youth, but with a chin that
spoke for much firmness of character. A
fur toque perched a little to one side gave
her a boyish air.

This undoubtedly was Shaver's mother
who had caught him prowling in her
house, and all The Hopper's plans for

74

explaining her son's disappearance and
returning him in a manner to win praise
and gratitude went glimmering. There was
nothing in the appearance of this Muriel
to encourage a hope that she was either
embarrassed or alarmed by his presence.
He had been captured many times, but the
trick had never been turned by any one
so cool as this young woman. She seemed
to be pondering with the greatest calmness what disposition she should make of
him. In the intentness of her thought
the revolver wavered for an instant, and
The Hopper, without taking his eyes from
her, made a cat-like spring that brought
him to the window he had raised against
just such an emergency.

"None of that!" she cried, walking
slowly toward him without lowering the
pistol. "If you attempt to jump from

that window I'll shoot! But it's cold in here and you may lower it."

The Hopper, weighing the chances, decided that the odds were heavily against escape, and lowered the window.

"Now," said Muriel, "step into that corner and keep your hands up where I can watch them."

The Hopper obeyed her instructions strictly. There was a telephone on the table near her and he expected her to summon help; but to his surprise she calmly seated herself, resting her right elbow on the arm of the chair, her head slightly tilted to one side, as she inspected him with greater attention along the blueblack barrel of her automatic. Unless he made a dash for liberty this extraordinary woman would, at her leisure, turn him over to the police as a housebreaker and his peaceful life as a chicken farmer would be at an end. Her prolonged silence troubled The Hopper. He had not been more nervous when waiting for the report of the juries which at times had passed upon his conduct, or for judges to fix his term of imprisonment.

"Yes'm," he muttered, with a view to ending a silence that had become intolerable.

Her eyes danced to the accompaniment of her thoughts, but in no way did she betray the slightest perturbation.

"I ain't done nothin'; hones' to God, I ain't!" he protested brokenly.

"I saw you through the window when you entered this room and I was watching while you read that note," said his captor. "I thought it funny that you should do that instead of packing up the

77

silver. Do you mind telling me just why you read that note?"

"Well, miss, I jes' thought it kind o' funny there wuz n't nobody round an' the letter was layin' there all open, an' I did n't see no harm in lookin'."

"It was awfully clever of you to crawl into the corner so nobody could see your light from the windows," she said with a tinge of admiration. "I suppose you thought you might find out how long the people of the house were likely to be gone and how much time you could spend here. Was that it?"

"I reckon ut wuz somethin' like that," he agreed.

This was received with the noncommittal "Um" of a person whose thoughts are elsewhere. Then, as though she were eliciting from an artist or man of letters a frank opinion as to his own ideas of his attainments and professional standing, she asked, with a meditative air that puzzled him as much as her question: —

"Just how good a burglar are you? Can you do a job neatly and safely?"

The Hopper, staggered by her inquiry and overcome by modesty, shrugged his shoulders and twisted about uncomfortably.

"I reckon as how you've pinched me I ain't much good," he replied, and was rewarded with a smile followed by a light little laugh. He was beginning to feel pleased that she manifested no fear of him. In fact, he had decided that Shaver's mother was the most remarkable woman he had ever encountered, and by all odds the handsomest. He began to take heart. Perhaps after all he might hit

upon some way of restoring Shaver to his
proper place in the house of Talbot without making himself liable to a long term
for kidnaping.

"If you're really a successful burglar
— one who does n't just poke around in
empty houses as you were doing here, but
clever and brave enough to break into
houses where people are living and steal
things without making a mess of it; and
if you can play fair about it — then I
think — I think — maybe — we can come
to terms!"

"Yes'm!" faltered The Hopper, beginning to wonder if Mary and Humpy had
been right in saying that he had lost his
mind. He was so astonished that his arms
wavered, but she was instantly on her feet
and the little automatic was again on a
level with his eyes.

A Reversible Santa Claus

"Excuse me, miss, I did n't mean to
drop 'em. I were n't goin' to do nothin'.
Hones' I wuz n't!" he pleaded with real
contrition. "It jes' seemed kind o' funny
what ye said."

He grinned sheepishly. If she knew
that her Billie, *alias* Shaver, was not with
her husband at his father's house, she
would not be dallying in this fashion.
And if the young father, who painted pictures, and left notes in his studio in a
blind faith that his wife would find them,
— if that trusting soul knew that Billie
was asleep in a house all of whose inmates
had done penance behind prison bars, he
would very quickly become a man of action. The Hopper had never heard of such
careless parenthood! These people were
children! His heart warmed to them in pity
and admiration, as it had to little Billie.

81

"I forgot to ask you whether you are armed," she remarked, with just as much composure as though she were asking him whether he took two lumps of sugar in his tea; and then she added, "I suppose I ought to have asked you that in the first place."

"I gotta gun in my coat—right side," he confessed. "An' that's all I got," he added, batting his eyes under the spell of her bewildering smile.

With her left hand she cautiously extracted his revolver and backed away with it to the table.

"If you'd lied to me I should have killed you; do you understand?"

"Yes'm," murmured The Hopper meekly.

She had spoken as though homicide were a common incident of her life, but a gleam of humor in the eyes she was watching vigilantly abated her severity.

"You may sit down — there, please!"

She pointed to a much bepillowed davenport and The Hopper sank down on it, still with his hands up. To his deepening mystification she backed to the windows and lowered the shades, and this done she sat down with the table between them, remarking, —

"You may put your hands down now, Mr. ——?"

He hesitated, decided that it was unwise to give any of his names; and respecting his scruples she said with great magnanimity: —

"Of course you wouldn't want to tell me your name, so don't trouble about that."

She sat, wholly tranquil, her arms upon the table, both hands caressing the small

automatic, while his own revolver, of different pattern and larger caliber, lay close
by. His status was now established as that
of a gentleman making a social call upon
a lady who, in the pleasantest manner
imaginable and yet with undeniable reso-
luteness, kept a deadly weapon pointed
in the general direction of his person.

A clock on the mantel struck eleven
with a low, silvery note. Muriel waited
for the last stroke and then spoke crisply
and directly.

"We were speaking of that letter I left
lying here on the table. You did n't understand it, of course; you could n't —
not really. So I will explain it to you.
My husband and I married against our
fathers' wishes; both of them were op-
posed to it."

She waited for this to sink into his

perturbed consciousness. The Hopper frowned and leaned forward to express his sympathetic interest in this confidential disclosure.

"My father," she resumed, "is just as stupid as my father-in-law and they have both continued to make us just as uncomfortable as possible. The cause of the trouble is ridiculous. There's nothing against my husband or me, you understand; it's simply a bitter jealousy between the two men due to the fact that they are rival collectors."

The Hopper stared blankly. The only collectors with whom he had enjoyed any acquaintance were persons who presented bills for payment.

"They are collectors," Muriel hastened to explain, "of ceramics — precious porcelains and that sort of thing."

"Yes'm," assented The Hopper, who had n't the faintest notion of what she meant.

"For years, whenever there have been important sales of these things, which men fight for and are willing to die for — whenever there has been something specially fine in the market, my father-in-law — he's Mr. Talbot — and Mr. Wilton — he's my father — have bid for them. There are auctions, you know, and people come from all over the world looking for a chance to buy the rarest pieces. They've explored China and Japan hunting for prizes and they are experts — men of rare taste and judgment — what you call connoisseurs."

The Hopper nodded gravely at the unfamiliar word, convinced that not only were Muriel and her husband quite in-

sane, but that they had inherited the in-
firmity.

"The trouble has been," Muriel continued, "that Mr. Talbot and my father
both like the same kind of thing; and
when one has got something the other
wanted, of course it has added to the ill-
feeling. This has been going on for years
and recently they have grown more bitter. When Roger and I ran off and got
married, that did n't help matters any;
but just within a few days something has
happened to make things much worse
than ever."

The Hopper's complete absorption in
this novel recital was so manifest that
she put down the revolver with which she
had been idling and folded her hands.

"Thank ye, miss," mumbled The Hopper.

"Only last week," Muriel continued, "my father-in-law bought one of those pottery treasures — a plum-blossom vase made in China hundreds of years ago and very, very valuable. It belonged to a Philadelphia collector who died not long ago and Mr. Talbot bought it from the executor of the estate, who happened to be an old friend of his. Father was very angry, for he had been led to believe that this vase was going to be offered at auction and he'd have a chance to bid on it. And just before that father had got hold of a jar — a perfectly wonderful piece of red Lang-Yao — that collectors everywhere have coveted for years. This made Mr. Talbot furious at father. My husband is at his father's now trying to make him see the folly of all this, and I visited *my* father to-day to try to persuade him to stop being so foolish. You see I wanted us all to be happy for Christmas! Of course, Christmas ought to be a time of gladness for everybody. Even people in your — er — profession must feel that Christmas is one day in the year when all hard feelings should be forgotten and everybody should try to make others happy."

"I guess yer right, miss. Ut sure seems foolish fer folks t' git mad about jugs like you says. Wuz they empty, miss?"

"Empty!" repeated Muriel wonderingly, not understanding at once that her visitor was unaware that the "jugs" men fought over were valued as art treasures and not for their possible contents. Then she laughed merrily, as only the mother of Shaver could laugh.

"Oh! Of course they're *empty!* That

does seem to make it sillier, does n't it? But they're like famous pictures, you know, or any beautiful work of art that only happens occasionally. Perhaps it seems odd to you that men can be so crazy about such things, but I suppose sometimes *you* have wanted things very, very much, and — oh!''

She paused, plainly confused by her tactlessness in suggesting to a member of his profession the extremities to which one may be led by covetousness.

''Yes, miss,'' he remarked hastily; and he rubbed his nose with the back of his hand, and grinned indulgently as he realized the cause of her embarrassment. It crossed his mind that she might be playing a trick of some kind; that her story, which seemed to him wholly fantastic and not at all like a chronicle of the acts of veritable human beings, was merely a device for detaining him until help arrived. But he dismissed this immediately as unworthy of one so pleasing, so beautiful, so perfectly qualified to be the mother of Shaver!

"Well, just before luncheon, without telling my husband where I was going, I ran away to papa's, hoping to persuade him to end this silly feud. I spent the afternoon there and he was very unreasonable. He feels that Mr. Talbot was n't fair about that Philadelphia purchase, and I gave it up and came home. I got here a little after dark and found my husband had taken Billie — that's our little boy — and gone. I knew, of course, that he had gone to *his* father's hoping to bring him round, for both our fathers are simply crazy about Billie. But you see I never go to Mr. Talbot's and my husband never goes — Dear me!" she broke off suddenly. "I suppose I ought to tele-phone and see if Billie is all right."

The Hopper, greatly alarmed, thrust his head forward as she pondered this. If she telephoned to her father-in-law's to ask about Billie, the jig would be up! He drew his hand across his face and fell back with relief as she went on, a little absently: —

"Mr. Talbot hates telephoning, and it might be that my husband is just getting him to the point of making concessions, and I should n't want to interrupt. It's so late now that of course Roger and Billie will spend the night there. And Billie and Christmas ought to be a combin-ation that would soften the hardest heart! You ought to see — you just ought to see

A Reversible Santa Claus

Billie! He's the cunningest, dearest baby in the world!"

The Hopper sat pigeon-toed, beset by countless conflicting emotions. His ingenuity was taxed to its utmost by the demands of this complex situation. But for his returning suspicion that Muriel was leading up to something; that she was detaining him for some purpose not yet apparent, he would have told her of her husband's note and confessed that the adored Billie was at that moment enjoying the reluctant hospitality of Happy Hill Farm. He resolved to continue his policy of silence as to the young heir's whereabouts until Muriel had shown her hand. She had not wholly abandoned the thought of telephoning to her father-in-law's, he found, from her next remark.

"You think it's all right, don't you?

A Reversible Santa Claus

It's strange Roger did n't leave me a note
of some kind. Our cook left a week ago
and there was no one here when he left."

"I reckon as how yer kid's all right,
miss," he answered consolingly.

Her voluble confidences had enthralled
him, and her reference of this matter to
his judgment was enormously flattering.
On the rough edges of society where he
had spent most of his life, fellow crafts-
men had frequently solicited his advice,
chiefly as to the disposition of their ill-
gotten gains or regarding safe harbors of
refuge, but to be taken into counsel by the
only gentlewoman he had ever met roused
his self-respect, touched a chivalry that
never before had been wakened in The
Hopper's soul. She was so like a child in
her guilelessness, and so brave amid her
perplexities!

A Reversible Santa Claus

"Oh, I know Roger will take beautiful
care of Billie. And now," she smiled
radiantly, "you're probably wondering
what I've been driving at all this time.
Maybe" — she added softly — "maybe
it's providential, your turning up here in
this way!"

She uttered this happily, with a little note of triumph and another of her
smiles that seemed to illuminate the uni-
verse. The Hopper had been called many
names in his varied career, but never before had he been invested with the attri-
butes of an agent of Providence.

"They's things wot is an' they's things
wot ain't, miss; I reckon I ain't as bad
as some. I mean to be on the square,
miss."

"I believe that," she said. "I've always heard there's honor among thieves,

and " — she lowered her voice to a whisper — "it's possible I might become one myself!"

The Hopper's eyes opened wide and he crossed and uncrossed his legs nervously in his agitation.

"If — if" — she began slowly, bending forward with a grave, earnest look in her eyes and clasping her fingers tightly — "if we could only get hold of father's Lang-Yao jar and that plum-blossom vase Mr. Talbot has — if we could only do that!"

The Hopper swallowed hard. This fearless, pretty young woman was calmly suggesting that he commit two felonies, little knowing that his score for the day already aggregated three — purse-snatching, the theft of an automobile from her own door, and what might very readily be construed as the kidnaping of her own child!

"I don't know, miss," he said feebly, calculating that the sum total of even minimum penalties for the five crimes would outrun his natural life and consume an eternity of reincarnations.

"Of course it would n't be stealing in the ordinary sense," she explained. "What I want you to do is to play the part of what we will call a reversible Santa Claus, who takes things away from stupid people who don't enjoy them anyhow. And maybe if they lost these things they'd behave themselves. I could explain afterward that it was all my fault, and of course I would n't let any harm come to *you*. I'd be responsible, and of course I'd see you safely out of it; you would have to rely on me for that. I'm trusting *you* and you'd have to trust *me!*"

"Oh, I'd trust ye, miss! An' ef I was to get pinched I would n't never squeal on ye. We don't never blab on a pal, miss!"

He was afraid she might resent being called a "pal," but his use of the term apparently pleased her.

"We understand each other, then. It really won't be very difficult, for papa's place is over on the Sound and Mr. Talbot's is right next to it, so you would n't have far to go."

Her utter failure to comprehend the enormity of the thing she was proposing affected him queerly. Even among hardened criminals in the underworld such undertakings are suggested cautiously; but Muriel was ordering a burglary as though it were a pound of butter or a dozen eggs!

"Father keeps his most valuable glazes in a safe in the pantry," she resumed after a moment's reflection, "but I can give you the combination. That will make it a lot easier."

The Hopper assented, with a pontifical nod, to this sanguine view of the matter.

"Mr. Talbot keeps his finest pieces in a cabinet built into the bookshelves in his library. It's on the left side as you stand in the drawing-room door, and you look for the works of Thomas Carlyle. There's a dozen or so volumes of Carlyle, only they're not books, — not really, — but just the backs of books painted on the steel of a safe. And if you press a spring in the upper right-hand corner of the shelf just over these books the whole section swings out. I suppose you've seen that sort of hiding-place for valuables?"

"Well, not exactly, miss. But havin' a tip helps, an' ef there ain't no soup to pour —"

"Soup?" inquired Muriel, wrinkling her pretty brows.

"That's the juice we pour into the cracks of a safe to blow out the lid with," The Hopper elucidated. "Ut's a lot handier ef you've got the combination. Ut usually ain't jes' layin' around."

"I should hope not!" exclaimed Muriel.

She took a sheet of paper from the leathern stationery rack and fell to scribbling, while he furtively eyed the window and again put from him the thought of flight.

"There! That's the combination of

papa's safe." She turned her wrist and glanced at her watch. "It's half-past eleven and you can catch a trolley in ten minutes that will take you right past papa's house. The butler's an old man who forgets to lock the windows half the time, and there's one in the conservatory with a broken catch. I noticed it to-day when I was thinking about stealing the jar myself!"

They were established on so firm a basis of mutual confidence that when he rose and walked to the table she did n't lift her eyes from the paper on which she was drawing a diagram of her father's house. He stood watching her nimble fingers, fascinated by the boldness of her plan for restoring amity between Shaver's grandfathers, and filled with admiration for her resourcefulness.

He asked a few questions as to exits and entrances and fixed in his mind a very accurate picture of the home of her father. She then proceeded to enlighten him as to the ways and means of entering the home of her father-in-law, which she sketched with equal facility.

"There's a French window — a narrow glass door — on the veranda. I think you might get in *there!*" She made a jab with the pencil. "Of course I should hate awfully to have you get caught! But you must have had a lot of experience, and with all the help I'm giving you — !"

A sudden lifting of her head gave him the full benefit of her eyes and he averted his gaze reverently.

"There's always a chance o' bein' nabbed, miss," he suggested with feeling.

Shaver's mother wielded the same hypnotic power, highly intensified, that he had felt in Shaver. He knew that he was going to attempt what she asked; that he was committed to the project of robbing two houses merely to please a pretty young woman who invited his coöperation at the point of a revolver!

"Papa's always a sound sleeper," she was saying. "When I was a little girl a burglar went all through our house and carried off his clothes and he never knew it until the next morning. But you'll have to be careful at Mr. Talbot's, for he suffers horribly from insomnia."

"They got any o' them fancy burglar alarms?" asked The Hopper as he concluded his examination of her sketches.

"Oh, I forgot to tell you about that!" she cried contritely. "There's nothing of the kind at Mr. Talbot's, but at papa's

there's a switch in the living-room, right
back of a bust — a white marble thing
on a pedestal. You turn it off *there*. Half
the time papa forgets to switch it on
before he goes to bed. And another thing
— be careful about stumbling over that
bearskin rug in the hall. People are always sticking their feet into its jaws."

"I'll look out for ut, miss."

Burglar alarms and the jaws of wild
beasts were not inviting hazards. The
programme she outlined so light-heart-
edly was full of complexities. It was
almost pathetic that any one could so
cheerfully and irresponsibly suggest the
perpetration of a crime. The terms she
used in describing the loot he was to filch
were much stranger to him than Chinese,
but it was fairly clear that at the Talbot
house he was to steal a blue-and-white

104

thing and at the Wilton's a red one. The form and size of these articles she illustrated with graceful gestures.

"If I thought you were likely to make a mistake I'd — I'd go with you!" she declared.

"Oh, no, miss; ye could n't do that! I guess I can do ut fer ye. Ut's jes' a *leetle* ticklish. I reckon ef yer pa wuz to nab me ut'd go hard with me."

"I would n't let him be hard on you," she replied earnestly. "And now I have n't said anything about a — a — about what we will call a *reward* for bringing me these porcelains. I shall expect to pay you; I could n't think of taking up your time, you know, for nothing!"

"Lor', miss, I could n't take nothin' at all fer doin' ut! Ye see ut wuz sort of accidental our meetin', and besides, I ain't no housebreaker — not, as ye may say, reg'ler. I'll be glad to do ut fer ye, miss, an' ye can rely on me doin' my best fer ye. Ye've treated me right, miss, an' I ain't a-goin' t' fergit ut!"

The Hopper spoke with feeling. Shaver's mother had, albeit at the pistol point, confided her most intimate domestic affairs to him. He realized, without finding just these words for it, that she had in effect decorated him with the symbol of her order of knighthood and he had every honorable — or dishonorable! — intention of proving himself worthy of her confidence.

"If ye please, miss," he said, pointing toward his confiscated revolver.

"Certainly; you may take it. But of course you won't *kill* anybody?"

"No, miss; only I'm sort o' lonesome without ut when I'm on a job."

"And you do understand," she said, following him to the door and noting in the distance the headlight of an approaching trolley, "that I'm only doing this in the hope that good may come of it. It isn't really criminal, you know; if you succeed, it may mean the happiest Christmas of my life!"

"Yes, miss. I won't come back till mornin', but don't you worry none. We gotta play safe, miss, an' ef I land th' jugs I'll find cover till I kin deliver 'em safe."

"Thank you; oh, thank you ever so much! And good luck!"

She put out her hand; he held it gingerly for a moment in his rough fingers and ran for the car.

VII

VII

THE HOPPER, in his rôle of the Reversible Santa Claus, dropped off the car at the crossing Muriel had carefully described, waited for the car to vanish, and warily entered the Wilton estate through a gate set in the stone wall. The clouds of the early evening had passed and the stars marched through the heavens resplendently, proclaiming peace on earth and good-will toward men. They were almost oppressively brilliant, seen through the clear, cold atmosphere, and as The Hopper slipped from one big tree to another on his tangential course to the house, he fortified his courage by muttering, "They's things wot is an' things wot ain't!" — finding much comfort and stimulus in the phrase.

Arriving at the conservatory in due course, he found that Muriel's averments as to the vulnerability of that corner of her father's house were correct in every particular. He entered with ease, sniffed the warm, moist air, and, leaving the door slightly ajar, sought the pantry, lowered the shades, and, helping himself to a candle from a silver candelabrum, readily found the safe hidden away in one of the cupboards. He was surprised to find himself more nervous with the combination in his hand than on memorable occasions in the old days when he had broken into country postoffices and assaulted safes

by force. In his haste he twice failed to
give the proper turns, but the third time
the knob caught, and in a moment the
door swung open disclosing shelves filled
with vases, bottles, bowls, and plates in
bewildering variety. A chest of silver ap-
pealed to him distractingly as a much
more tangible asset than the pottery, and
he dizzily contemplated a jewel-case containing a diamond necklace with a pearl
pendant. The moment was a critical one
in The Hopper's eventful career. This daz-
zling prize was his for the taking, and he
knew the operator of a fence in Chicago
who would dispose of the necklace and
make him a fair return. But visions of
Muriel, the beautiful, the confiding, and of
her little Shaver asleep on Humpy's bed,
rose before him. He steeled his heart
against temptation, drew his candle along

113

the shelf and scrutinized the glazes. There could be no mistaking the red Lang-Yao whose brilliant tints kindled in the candle-glow. He lifted it tenderly, verifying the various points of Muriel's description, set it down on the floor and locked the safe.

He was retracing his steps toward the conservatory and had reached the main hall when the creaking of the stairsteps brought him up with a start. Some one was descending, slowly and cautiously. For a second time and with grateful appreciation of Muriel's forethought, he carefully avoided the ferocious jaws of the bear, noiselessly continued on to the conservatory, crept through the door, closed it, and then, crouching on the steps, awaited developments. The caution exercised by the person descending the

stairway was not that of a householder
who has been roused from slumber by a
disquieting noise. The Hopper was keenly
interested in this fact.

With his face against the glass he
watched the actions of a tall, elderly man
with a short, grayish beard, who wore a
golf-cap pulled low on his head — points
noted by The Hopper in the flashes of an
electric lamp with which the gentleman
was guiding himself. His face was clearly
the original of a photograph The Hopper
had seen on the table at Muriel's cottage
— Mr. Wilton, Muriel's father, The Hopper surmised; but just why the owner
of the establishment should be prowling
about in this fashion taxed his specula-
tive powers to the utmost. Warned by
steps on the cement floor of the conservatory, he left the door in haste and flat-

tened himself against the wall of the house some distance away and again awaited developments.

Wilton's figure was a blur in the starlight as he stepped out into the walk and started furtively across the grounds. His conduct greatly displeased The Hopper, as likely to interfere with the further carrying out of Muriel's instructions. The Lang-Yao jar was much too large to go into his pocket and not big enough to fit snugly under his arm, and as the walk was slippery he was beset by the fear that he might fall and smash this absurd thing that had caused so bitter an enmity between Shaver's grandfathers. The soft snow on the lawn gave him a surer footing and he crept after Wilton, who was carefully pursuing his way toward a house whose gables were faintly limned against

THE FAINT CLICK OF A LATCH MARKED THE PROWLER'S
PROXIMITY TO A HEDGE

the sky. This, according to Muriel's diagram, was the Talbot place. The Hopper
greatly mistrusted conditions he did n't
understand, and he was at a loss to account for Wilton's strange actions.

He lost sight of him for several minutes, then the faint click of a latch marked
the prowler's proximity to a hedge that
separated the two estates. The Hopper
crept forward, found a gate through which
Wilton had entered his neighbor's property, and stole after him. Wilton had
been swallowed up by the deep shadow of
the house, but The Hopper was aware,
from an occasional scraping of feet, that he
was still moving forward. He crawled over
the snow until he reached a large tree
whose boughs, sharply limned against the
stars, brushed the eaves of the house.

The Hopper was aroused, tremendously

aroused, by the unaccountable actions of
Muriel's father. It flashed upon him that
Wilton, in his deep hatred of his rival collector, was about to set fire to Talbot's
house, and incendiarism was a crime
which The Hopper, with all his moral
obliquity, greatly abhorred.

Several minutes passed, a period of anxious waiting, and then a sound reached
him which, to his keen professional sense,
seemed singularly like the forcing of a window. The Hopper knew just how much
pressure is necessary to the successful
snapping back of a window catch, and Wilton had done the trick neatly and with
a minimum amount of noise. The window thus assaulted was not, he now de-
termined, the French window suggested
by Muriel, but one opening on a terrace
which ran along the front of the house.

A Reversible Santa Claus

The Hopper heard the sash moving slowly in the frame. He reached the steps, deposited the jar in a pile of snow, and was soon peering into a room where Wilton's presence was advertised by the fitful flashing of his lamp in a far corner.

"He's beat me to ut!" muttered The Hopper, realizing that Muriel's father was indeed on burglary bent, his obvious purpose being to purloin, extract, and remove from its secret hiding-place the coveted plum-blossom vase. Muriel, in her longing for a Christmas of peace and happiness, had not reckoned with her father's passionate desire to possess the porcelain treasure — a desire which could hardly fail to cause scandal, if it did not land him behind prison bars.

This had not been in the programme, and The Hopper weighed judicially his

further duty in the matter. Often as he
had been the chief actor in daring rob-
beries, he had never before enjoyed the
high privilege of watching a rival's labors
with complete detachment. Wilton must
have known of the concealed cupboard
whose panel fraudulently represented the
works of Thomas Carlyle, the intent
spectator reflected, just as Muriel had
known, for though he used his lamp
sparingly Wilton had found his way to
it without difficulty.

The Hopper had no intention of per-
mitting this monstrous larceny to be
committed in contravention of his own
rights in the premises, and he was con-
sidering the best method of wresting the
vase from the hands of the insolent Wilton when events began to multiply with
startling rapidity. The panel swung open

120

and the thief's lamp flashed upon shelves
of pottery.

At that moment a shout rose from
somewhere in the house, and the library
lights were thrown on, revealing Wilton
before the shelves and their precious contents. A short, stout gentleman with a
gleaming bald pate, clad in pajamas,
dashed across the room, and with a yell
of rage flung himself upon the intruder
with a violence that bore them both to
the floor.

"Roger! Roger!" bawled the smaller
man, as he struggled with his adversary,
who wriggled from under and rolled over
upon Talbot, whose arms were clasped
tightly about his neck. This embrace
seemed likely to continue for some time,
so tenaciously had the little man gripped
his neighbor. The fat legs of the infuri-

ated householder pawed the air as he hugged Wilton, who was now trying to free his head and gain a position of greater dignity. Occasionally, as opportunity offered, the little man yelled vociferously, and from remote recesses of the house came answering cries demanding information as to the nature and whereabouts of the disturbance.

The contestants addressed themselves vigorously to a spirited rough-and-tumble fight. Talbot, who was the more easily observed by reason of his shining pate and the pink stripes of his pajamas, appeared to be revolving about the person of his neighbor. Wilton, though taller, lacked the rotund Talbot's liveliness of attack.

An authoritative voice, which The Hopper attributed to Shaver's father, anxiously demanding what was the matter, terminated The Hopper's enjoyment of the struggle. Enough was the matter to satisfy The Hopper that a prolonged stay in the neighborhood might be highly detrimental to his future liberty. The combatants had rolled a considerable distance away from the shelves and were near a door leading into a room beyond. A young man in a bath-wrapper dashed upon the scene, and in his precipitate arrival upon the battle-field fell sprawling across the prone figures. The Hopper, suddenly inspired to deeds of prowess, crawled through the window, sprang past the three men, seized the blue-and-white vase which Wilton had separated from the rest of Talbot's treasures, and then with one hop gained the window. As he turned for a last look, a pistol

123

cracked and he landed upon the terrace amid a shower of glass from a shattered pane.

A woman of unmistakable Celtic origin screamed murder from a third-story window. The thought of murder was disagreeable to The Hopper. Shaver's father had missed him by only the matter of a foot or two, and as he had no intention of offering himself again as a target he stood not upon the order of his going.

He effected a running pick-up of the Lang-Yao, and with this art treasure under one arm and the plum-blossom vase under the other, he sprinted for the highway, stumbling over shrubbery, bumping into a stone bench that all but caused disaster, and finally reached the road on which he continued his flight toward New Haven, followed by cries in many keys and a fusillade of pistol shots.

Arriving presently at a hamlet, where he paused for breath in the rear of a country store, he found a basket and a quantity of paper in which he carefully packed his loot. Over the top he spread some faded lettuce leaves and discarded carnations which communicated something of a blithe holiday air to his encumbrance. Elsewhere he found a bicycle under a shed, and while cycling over a snowy road in the dark, hampered by a basket containing pottery representative of the highest genius of the Orient, was not without its difficulties and dangers, The Hopper made rapid progress.

Halfway through New Haven he approached two policemen and slowed down to allay suspicion.

"Merry Chris'mas!" he called as he passed them and increased his weight upon the pedals.

The officers of the law, cheered as by a greeting from Santa Claus himself, responded with an equally hearty Merry Christmas.

VIII

VIII

At three o'clock The Hopper reached Happy Hill Farm, knocked as before at the kitchen door, and was admitted by Humpy.

"Wot ye got now?" snarled the reformed yeggman.

"He's gone and done ut ag'in!" wailed Mary, as she spied the basket.

"I sure done ut, all right," admitted The Hopper good-naturedly, as he set the basket on the table where a few hours earlier he had deposited Shaver. "How's the kid?"

Grudging assurances that Shaver was asleep and hostile glances directed at the mysterious basket did not disturb his equanimity.

Humpy was thwarted in an attempt to pry into the contents of the basket by a tart reprimand from The Hopper, who with maddening deliberation drew forth the two glazes, found that they had come through the night's vicissitudes unscathed, and held them at arm's length, turning them about in leisurely fashion as though lost in admiration of their loveliness. Then he lighted his pipe, seated himself in Mary's rocker, and told his story.

It was no easy matter to communicate to his irritable and contumelious auditors the sense of Muriel's charm, or the reasonableness of her request that he commit burglary merely to assist her in settling a family row. Mary could not understand it; Humpy paced the room nervously, shaking his head and muttering. It was their judgment, stated with much frankness, that if he had been a fool in the first place to steal the child, his character was now blackened beyond any hope by his later crimes. Mary wept copiously; Humpy most annoyingly kept counting upon his fingers as he reckoned the "time" that was in store for all of them.

"I guess I got into ut an' I guess I'll git out," remarked The Hopper serenely. He was disposed to treat them with high condescension, as incapable of appreciating the lofty philosophy of life by which he was sustained. Meanwhile, he gloated over the loot of the night.

A Reversible Santa Claus

"Them things is wurt' mints; they's
more valible than di'mon's, them things
is! Only eddicated folks knows about
'em. They's fer emp'rors and kings t' set
up in their palaces, an' men goes nutty
jes' hankerin' fer 'em. The pigtails made
'em thousand o' years back, an' th' secret
died with 'em. They ain't never goin' to
be no more jugs like them settin' right
there. An' them two ole sports give up
their business jes' t' chase things like
them. They's some folks goes loony
about chickens, an' hosses, an' fancy dogs,
but this here kind o' collectin' 's only fer
millionaires. They's more difficult t' pick
than a lucky race-hoss. They's barrels o'
that stuff in them houses, that looked jes'
as good as them there, but nowheres as
valible."

An informal lecture on Chinese ceram-

ics before daylight on Christmas morning was not to the liking of the anxious
and nerve-torn Mary and Humpy. They
brought The Hopper down from his lofty
heights to practical questions touching
his plans, for the disposal of Shaver in the
first instance, and the ceramics in the
second. The Hopper was singularly un-
moved by their forebodings.

"I guess th' lady got me to do ut!" he
retorted finally. "Ef I do time fer ut I
reckon's how she's in fer ut, too! An'
I seen her pap breakin' into a house an' I
guess I'd be a state's witness fer that! I
reckon they ain't goin' t' put nothin' over
on Hop! I guess they won't peep much
about kidnapin' with th' kid safe an' us
pickin' 'im up out o' th' road an' shelterin'
'im. Them folks is goin' to be awful nice
to Hop fer all he done fer 'em." And

then, finding that they were impressed by his defense, thus elaborated, he magnanimously referred to the bill-book which had started him on his downward course.

"That were a mistake; I grant ye ut were a mistake o' jedgment. I'm goin' to keep to th' white card. But ut's kind o' funny about that poke — queerest thing that ever happened."

He drew out the book and eyed the name on the flap. Humpy tried to grab it, but The Hopper, frustrating the attempt, read his colleague a sharp lesson in good manners. He restored it to his pocket and glanced at the clock.

"We gotta do somethin' about Shaver's stockin's. Ut ain't fair fer a kid to wake up an' think Santy missed 'im. Ye got some candy, Mary; we kin put candy into 'em; that's reg'ler."

134

A Reversible Santa Claus

Humpy brought in Shaver's stockings
and they were stuffed with the candy
and popcorn Mary had provided to adorn
their Christmas feast. Humpy invento-
ried his belongings, but could think of
nothing but a revolver that seemed a
suitable gift for Shaver. This Mary
scornfully rejected as improper for one so
young. Whereupon Humpy produced a
Mexican silver dollar, a treasured pocket-
piece preserved through many tribula-
tions, and dropped it reverently into one
of the stockings. Two brass buttons of
unknown history, a mouth-organ Mary
had bought for a neighbor boy who as-
sisted at times in the poultry yard, and a
silver spectacle case of uncertain antece-
dents were added.

"We ought t' 'a' colored eggs fer 'im!"
said The Hopper with sudden inspiration,

after the stockings had been restored to Shaver's bed. "Some yaller an' pink eggs would 'a' been the right ticket."

Mary scoffed at the idea. Eggs was n't proper fer Christmas; eggs was fer Easter. Humpy added the weight of his personal experience of Christian holidays to this statement. While a trusty in the Missouri penitentiary with the chicken yard in his keeping, he remembered distinctly that eggs were in demand for purposes of decoration by the warden's children sometime in the spring; mebbe it was Easter, mebbe it was Decoration Day; Humpy was not sure of anything except that it was n't Christmas.

The Hopper was meek under correction. It having been settled that colored eggs would not be appropriate for Christmas he yielded to their demand that he show some enthusiasm for disposing of his ill-gotten treasures before the police arrived to take the matter out of his hands.

"I guess that Muriel'll be glad to see me," he remarked. "I guess me and her understands each other. They's things wot is an' things wot ain't; an' I guess Hop ain't goin' to spend no Chris'mas in jail. It's the white card an' poultry an' eggs fer us; an' we're goin' t' put in a couple more incubators right away. I'm thinkin' some o' rentin' that acre across th' brook back yonder an' raisin' tur-keys. They's mints in turks, ef ye kin keep 'em from gettin' their feet wet an' dyin' o' pneumonia, which wipes out thousands o' them birds. I reckon ye might make some coffee, Mary."

The Christmas dawn found them at the table, where they were renewing a

pledge to play "the white card" when a
cry from Shaver brought them to their
feet.

Shaver was highly pleased with his
Christmas stockings, but his pleasure
was nothing to that of The Hopper,
Mary, and Humpy, as they stood about
the bed and watched him. Mary and
Humpy were so relieved by The Hopper's
promises to lead a better life that they
were now disposed to treat their guest
with the most distinguished consideration.
Humpy, absenting himself to perform
his morning tasks in the poultry-houses,
returned bringing a basket containing six
newly hatched chicks. These cheeped and
ran over Shaver's fat legs and performed
exactly as though they knew they were
a part of his Christmas entertainment.
Humpy, proud of having thought of the

chicks, demanded the privilege of serving
Shaver's breakfast. Shaver ate his porridge without a murmur, so happy was he
over his new playthings.

Mary bathed and dressed him with
care. As the candy had stuck to the
stockings in spots, it was decided after a
family conference that Shaver would have
to wear them wrong side out as there was
no time to be wasted in washing them.
By eight o'clock The Hopper announced
that it was time for Shaver to go home.
Shaver expressed alarm at the thought
of leaving his chicks; whereupon Humpy
conferred two of them upon him in the
best imitation of baby talk that he could
muster.

"Me's tate um to me's gwanpas," said
Shaver; "chickee for me's two gwanpas,"
—a remark which caused The Hopper

to shake for a moment with mirth as he
recalled his last view of Shaver's "gwanpas" in a death grip upon the floor of
"Gwanpa" Talbot's house.

IX

IX

WHEN The Hopper rolled away from Happy Hill Farm in the stolen machine, accompanied by one stolen child and forty thousand dollars' worth of stolen pottery, Mary wept, whether because of the parting with Shaver, or because she feared that The Hopper would never return, was not clear.

Humpy, too, showed signs of tears, but concealed his weakness by performing a grotesque dance, dancing grotesquely by the side of the car, much to Shaver's joy — a joy enhanced just as the car reached the gate, where, as a farewell attention, Humpy fell down and rolled over and over in the snow.

The Hopper's wits were alert as he bore Shaver homeward. By this time it was likely that the confiding young Talbots had conferred over the telephone and knew that their offspring had disappeared. Doubtless the New Haven police had been notified, and he chose his route with discretion to avoid unpleasant encounters. Shaver, his spirits keyed to holiday pitch, babbled ceaselessly, and The Hopper, highly elated, babbled back at him.

They arrived presently at the rear of the young Talbots' premises, and The Hopper, with Shaver trotting at his side, advanced cautiously upon the house bearing the two baskets, one containing Shav-

er's chicks, the other the precious porcelains. In his survey of the landscape he
noted with trepidation the presence of
two big limousines in the highway in
front of the cottage and decided that if
possible he must see Muriel alone and
make his report to her.

The moment he entered the kitchen he
heard the clash of voices in angry dispute
in the living-room. Even Shaver was
startled by the violence of the conversa-
tion in progress within, and clutched
tightly a fold of The Hopper's trousers.

"I tell you it's John Wilton who has
stolen Billie!" a man cried tempestuously.
"Anybody who would enter a neighbor's
house in the dead of night and try to
rob him — rob him, yes, and *murder* him
in the most brutal fashion — would not
scruple to steal his own grandchild!"

A Reversible Santa Claus

"Me's gwanpa," whispered Shaver, gripping The Hopper's hand, "an' 'im's mad."

That Mr. Talbot was very angry indeed was established beyond cavil. However, Mr. Wilton was apparently quite capable of taking care of himself in the dispute.

"You talk about my stealing when you robbed me of my Lang-Yao — bribed my servants to plunder my safe! I want you to understand once for all, Roger Talbot, that if that jar is n't returned within one hour, — within one hour, sir, — I shall turn you over to the police!"

"Liar!" bellowed Talbot, who possessed a voice of great resonance. "You can't mitigate your foul crime by charging me with another! I never saw your jar; I never wanted it! I would n't have the thing on my place!"

146

Muriel's voice, full of tears, was lifted in expostulation.

"How can you talk of your silly vases when Billie's lost! Billie's been stolen — and you two men can think of nothing but pot-ter-ree!"

Shaver lifted a startled face to The Hopper.

"Mamma's cwyin'; gwanpa's hurted mamma!"

The strategic moment had arrived when Shaver must be thrust forward as an interruption to the exchange of disagreeable epithets by his grandfathers.

"You trot right in there t' yer ma, Shaver. Ole Hop ain't goin' t' let 'em hurt ye!"

He led the child through the dining-room to the living-room door and pushed him gently on the scene of strife. Talbot,

147

senior, was pacing the floor with angry strides, declaiming upon his wrongs, — indeed, his theme might have been the misery of the whole human race from the vigor of his lamentations. His son was keeping step with him, vainly attempting to persuade him to sit down. Wilton, with a patch over his right eye, was trying to disengage himself from his daughter's arms with the obvious intention of doing violence to his neighbor.

"I'm sure papa never meant to hurt you; it was all a dreadful mistake," she moaned.

"He had an accomplice," Talbot thundered, "and while he was trying to kill me there in my own house the plum-blossom vase was carried off; and if Roger had n't pushed him out of the window after his hireling — I'd — I'd —"

A Reversible Santa Claus

A shriek from Muriel happily prevented
the completion of a sentence that gave
every promise of intensifying the prevail-
ing hard feeling.

"Look!" Muriel cried. "It's Billie come
back! Oh, Billie!"

She sprang toward the door and clasped
the frightened child to her heart. The
three men gathered round them, staring
dully. The Hopper from behind the door
waited for Muriel's joy over Billie's return to communicate itself to his father
and the two grandfathers.

"Me's dot two chick-*ees* for Kwismus," announced Billie, wriggling in his
mother's arms.

Muriel, having satisfied herself that
Billie was intact, — that he even bore
the marks of maternal care, — was in the
act of transferring him to his bewildered

father, when, turning a tear-stained face toward the door, she saw The Hopper awkwardly twisting the derby which he had donned as proper for a morning call of ceremony. She walked toward him with quick, eager step.

"You — you came back!" she faltered, stifling a sob.

"Yes'm," responded The Hopper, rubbing his hand across his nose. His appearance roused Billie's father to a sense of his parental responsibility.

"You brought the boy back! You are the kidnaper!"

"Roger," cried Muriel protestingly, "don't speak like that! I'm sure this gentleman can explain how he came to bring Billie."

The quickness with which she regained her composure, the ease with which she

150

THE THREE MEN GATHERED ROUND THEM, STARING DULLY

adjusted herself to the unforeseen situation, pleased The Hopper greatly. He had not misjudged Muriel; she was an admirable ally, an ideal confederate. She gave him a quick little nod, as much as to say, "Go on, sir; we understand each other perfectly," — though, of course, she did not understand, nor was she enlightened until some time later, as to just how The Hopper became possessed of Billie.

Billie's father declared his purpose to invoke the law upon his son's kidnapers no matter where they might be found.

"I reckon as mebbe ut wuz a kidnapin' an' I reckon as mebbe ut wuz n't," The Hopper began unhurriedly. "I live over Shell Road way; poultry and eggs is my line; Happy Hill Farm. Stevens 's the name — Charles S. Stevens. An' I found

151

Shaver — 'scuse me, but ut seemed sort
o' nat'ral name fer 'im — I found 'im a
settin' up in th' machine over there by
my place, chipper's ye please. I takes 'im
into my house an' Mary — that's th'
missus — she gives 'im supper and puts
'im t' sleep. An' we thinks mebbe somebody'd come along askin' fer 'im. An'
then this mornin' I calls th' New Haven
police, an' they tole me about you folks,
an' me and Shaver comes right over."

This was entirely plausible and his
hearers, The Hopper noted with relief,
accepted it at face value.

"How dear of you!" cried Muriel.
"Won't you have this chair, Mr. Stevens!"

"Most remarkable!" exclaimed Wilton. "Some scoundrelly tramp picked up
the car and finding there was a baby in-

side left it at the roadside like the brute he was!"

Billie had addressed himself promptly to the Christmas tree, to his very own Christmas tree that was laden with gifts that had been assembled by the family for his delectation. Efforts of Grandfather Wilton to extract from the child some account of the man who had run away with him were unavailing. Billie was busy, very busy, indeed. After much patient effort he stopped sorting the animals in a bright new Noah's Ark to point his finger at The Hopper and remark: —

"'Ims nice mans; 'ims let Bil-lee play wif 'ims watch!"

As Billie had broken the watch his acknowledgment of The Hopper's courtesy in letting him play with it brought a grin to The Hopper's face.

A Reversible Santa Claus

Now that Billie had been returned
and his absence satisfactorily accounted
for, the two connoisseurs showed signs of
renewing their quarrel. Responsive to
a demand from Billie, The Hopper got
down on the floor to assist in the proper
mating of Noah's animals. Billie's father
was scrutinizing him fixedly and The Hopper wondered whether Muriel's handsome
young husband had recognized him as
the person who had vanished through
the window of the Talbot home bearing
the plum-blossom vase. The thought was
disquieting; but feigning deep interest in
the Ark he listened attentively to a vio-
lent tirade upon which the senior Talbot
was launched.

"My God!" he cried bitterly, planting
himself before Wilton in a belligerent
attitude, "every infernal thing that can

happen to a man happened to me yester-
day. It was n't enough that you robbed
me and tried to murder me — yes, you
did, sir! — but when I was in the city I
was robbed in the subway by a pick-
pocket. A thief took my bill-book containing invaluable data I had just received from my agent in China giving me
a clue to porcelains, sir, such as you never
dreamed of! Some more of your work —
Don't you contradict me! You don't
contradict me! Roger, he does n't contradict me!"

Wilton, choking with indignation at
this new onslaught, was unable to contradict him.

Pained by the situation, The Hopper
rose from the floor and coughed timidly.

"Shaver, go fetch yer chickies. Bring
yer chickies in an' put 'em on th' boat."

Billie obediently trotted off toward the kitchen and The Hopper turned his back upon the Christmas tree, drew out the pocket-book and faced the company.

"I beg yer pardon, gents, but mebbe this is th' book yer fightin' about. Kind o' funny like! I picked ut up on th' local yistiddy afternoon. I wuz goin' t' turn ut int' th' agint, but I clean fergot ut. I guess them papers may be valible. I never touched none of 'em."

Talbot snatched the bill-book and hastily examined the contents. His brow relaxed and he was grumbling something about a reward when Billie reappeared, laboriously dragging two baskets.

"Bil-lee's dot chick-*ees!* Bil-lee's dot pitty dishes. Bil-lee make dishes go 'ippity!"

Before he could make the two jars go

'ippity, The Hopper leaped across the room and seized the basket. He tore off the towel with which he had carefully covered the stolen pottery and disclosed the contents for inspection.

"'Scuse me, gents; no crowdin'," he warned as the connoisseurs sprang toward him. He placed the porcelains carefully on the floor under the Christmas tree. "Now ye kin listen t' me, gents. I reckon I'm goin' t' have somethin' t' say about this here crockery. I stole 'em — I stole 'em fer th' lady there, she thinkin' ef ye did n't have 'em no more ye'd stop rowin' about 'em. Ye kin call th' bulls an' turn me over ef ye likes; but I ain't goin' t' have ye fussin' an' causin' th' lady trouble no more. I ain't goin' to stand fer ut!"

"Robber!" shouted Talbot. "You entered my house at the instance of this man; it was you —"

"I never saw the gent before," declared The Hopper hotly. "I ain't never had nothin' to do with neither o' ye."

"He's telling the truth!" protested Muriel, laughing hysterically. "I did it — I got him to take them!"

The two collectors were not interested in explanations; they were hungrily eyeing their property. Wilton attempted to pass The Hopper and reach the Christmas tree under whose protecting boughs the two vases were looking their loveliest.

"Stand back," commanded The Hopper, "an' stop callin' names! I guess ef I'm yanked fer this I ain't th' only one that's goin' t' do time fer house breakin'."

This statement, made with considerable vigor, had a sobering effect upon

A Reversible Santa Claus

Wilton, but Talbot began dancing round the tree looking for a chance to pounce upon the porcelains.

"Ef ye don't set down — the whole caboodle o' ye — I'll smash 'em — I'll smash 'em both! I'll bust 'em — sure as shootin'!" shouted The Hopper.

They cowered before him; Muriel wept softly; Billie played with his chickies, disdainful of the world's woe. The Hopper, holding the two angry men at bay, was enjoying his command of the situation.

"You gents ain't got no business to be fussin' an' causin' yer childern trouble. An' ye ain't goin' to have these pretty jugs to fuss about no more. I'm goin' t' give 'em away; I'm goin' to make a Chris'mas present of 'em to Shaver. They're goin' to be little Shaver's right here, all orderly an' peace'ble, or I'll

159

tromp on 'em! Looky here, Shaver, wot Santy Claus brought ye!"

"Nice dood Sant' Claus!" cried Billie, diving under the davenport in quest of the wandering chicks.

Silence held the grown-ups. The Hopper stood patiently by the Christmas tree, awaiting the result of his diplomacy.

Then suddenly Wilton laughed — a loud laugh expressive of relief. He turned to Talbot and put out his hand.

"It looks as though Muriel and her friend here had cornered us! The idea of pooling our trophies and giving them as a Christmas present to Billie appeals to me strongly. And, besides we've got to prepare somebody to love these things after we're gone. We can work together and train Billie to be the greatest collector in America!"

160

A Reversible Santa Claus

"Please, father," urged Roger as Talbot frowned and shook his head impatiently.

Billie, struck with the happy thought of hanging one of his chickies on the Christmas tree, caused them all to laugh at this moment. It was difficult to refuse to be generous on Christmas morning in the presence of the happy child!

"Well," said Talbot, a reluctant smile crossing his face, "I guess it's all in the family anyway."

The Hopper, feeling that his work as the Reversible Santa Claus was finished. was rapidly retreating through the dining-room when Muriel and Roger ran after him.

"We're going to take you home," cried Muriel, beaming.

"Yer car's at the back gate, all right-

side-up," said The Hopper, "but I kin go
on the trolley."

"Indeed you won't! Roger will take
you home. Oh, don't be alarmed! My
husband knows everything about our
conspiracy. And we want you to come
back this afternoon. You know I owe you
an apology for thinking — for thinking
you were — you were — a —"

"They's things wot is an' things wot
ain't, miss. Circumstantial evidence sends
lots o' men to th' chair. Ut's a heap more
happy like," The Hopper continued in
his best philosophical vein, "t' play th'
white card, helpin' widders an' orfants an'
settlin' fusses. When ye ast me t' steal
them jugs I had n't th' heart t' refuse
ye, miss. I wuz scared to tell ye I had yer
baby an' ye seemed so sort o' trustin' like.
An' ut bein' Chris'mus an' all."

When he steadfastly refused to promise to return, Muriel announced that they would visit The Hopper late in the afternoon and bring Billie along to express their thanks more formally.

"I'll be glad to see ye," replied The Hopper, though a little doubtfully and shamefacedly. "But ye must n't git me into no more house-breakin' scrapes," he added with a grin. "It's mighty dangerous, miss, fer amachures, like me an' yer pa!"

X

X

MARY was not wholly pleased at the prospect of visitors, but she fell to work with Humpy to put the house in order. At five o'clock not one, but three automobiles drove into the yard, filling Humpy with alarm lest at last The Hopper's sins had overtaken him and they were all about to be hauled away to spend the rest of their lives in prison. It was not the police, but the young Talbots, with Billie and his grandfathers, on their way to a family celebration at the house of an aunt of Muriel's.

The grandfathers were restored to perfect amity, and were deeply curious now about The Hopper, whom the peace-loving Muriel had cajoled into robbing their houses.

"And you're only an honest chicken farmer, after all!" exclaimed Talbot, senior, when they were all sitting in a semicircle about the fireplace in Mary's parlor. "I hoped you were really a burglar; I always wanted to know a burglar."

Humpy had chopped down a small fir that had adorned the front yard and had set it up as a Christmas tree—an attention that was not lost upon Billie. The Hopper had brought some mechanical toys from town and Humpy essayed the agreeable task of teaching the youngster how to operate them. Mary produced coffee and pound cake for the guests; The Hopper assumed the rôle of lord of the manor with a benevolent air that was intended as much to impress Mary and Humpy as the guests.

"Of course," said Mr. Wilton, whose appearance was the least bit comical by reason of his bandaged head, — "of course it was very foolish for a man of your sterling character to allow a young woman like my daughter to bully you into robbing houses for her. Why, when Roger fired at you as you were jumping out of the window, he did n't miss you more than a foot! It would have been ghastly for all of us if he had killed you!"

"Well, o' course it all begun from my goin' into th' little house lookin' fer Shaver's folks," replied The Hopper.

"But you have n't told us how you came to find our house," said Roger, sug-

169

gesting a perfectly natural line of inquir-
ies that caused Humpy to become deeply
preoccupied with a pump he was operat-
ing in a basin of water for Billie's benefit.

"Well, ut jes' looked like a house that
Shaver would belong to, cute an' comfortable like," said The Hopper; "I jes' sus-
picioned it wuz th' place as I wuz passin'
along."

"I don't think we'd better begin trying to establish alibis," remarked Muriel,
very gently, "for we might get into terri-
ble scrapes. Why, if Mr. Stevens had n't
been so splendid about *everything* and
was n't just the kindest man in the world,
he could make it very ugly for *me*."

"I shudder to think of what he might
do to me," said Wilton, glancing guardedly at his neighbor.

"The main thing," said Talbot, —

"the main thing is that Mr. Stevens has done for us all what nobody else could ever have done. He's made us see how foolish it is to quarrel about mere baubles. He's settled all our troubles for us, and for my part I'll say his solution is entirely satisfactory."

"Quite right," ejaculated Wilton. "If I ever have any delicate business negotiations that are beyond my powers I'm going to engage Mr. Stevens to handle them."

"My business's hens an' eggs," said The Hopper modestly; "an' we're doin' purty well."

When they rose to go (a move that evoked strident protests from Billie, who was enjoying himself hugely with Humpy) they were all in the jolliest humor.

"We must be neighborly," said Muriel,

shaking hands with Mary, who was at the point of tears so great was her emotion at the success of The Hopper's party. "And we're going to buy all our chickens and eggs from you. We never have any luck raising our own."

Whereupon The Hopper imperturbably pressed upon each of the visitors a neat card stating his name (his latest and let us hope his last!) with the proper rural route designation of Happy Hill Farm.

The Hopper carried Billie out to his Grandfather Wilton's car, while Humpy walked beside him bearing the gifts from the Happy Hill Farm 'Christmas tree. From the door Mary watched them depart amid a chorus of merry Christmases, out of which Billie's little pipe rang cheerily.

When The Hopper and Humpy returned to the house, they abandoned the parlor for the greater coziness of the kitchen and there took account of the events of the momentous twenty-four hours.

"Them's what I call nice folks," said Humpy. "They jes' put us on an' wore us like we wuz a pair o' ole slippers."

"They wuz n't uppish — not to speak of," Mary agreed. "I guess that girl's got more gumption than any of 'em. She's got 'em straightened up now and I guess she'll take care they don't cut up no more monkey-shines about that Chinese stuff. Her husban' seemed sort o' gentle like."

"Artists is that way," volunteered The Hopper, as though from deep experience of art and life. "I jes' been thinkin' that knowin' folks like that an' findin' 'em

173

humin, makin' mistakes like th' rest of us,
kind o' makes ut seem easier fer us all t'
play th' game straight. Ut's goin' to be
th' white card fer me — jes' chickens an'
eggs, an' here's hopin' the bulls don't
ever find out we're settled here."

Humpy, having gone into the parlor to
tend the fire, returned with two envelopes
he had found on the mantel. There was
a check for a thousand dollars in each,
one from Wilton, the other from Talbot,
with "Merry Christmas" written across
the visiting-cards of those gentlemen.
The Hopper permitted Mary and Humpy
to examine them and then laid them on
the kitchen table, while he deliberated.
His meditations were so prolonged that
they grew nervous.

"I reckon they could spare ut, after all
ye done fer 'em, Hop," remarked Humpy.

174

A Reversible Santa Claus

"They's millionaires, an' money ain't nothin' to 'em," said The Hopper.

"We can buy a motor-truck," suggested Mary, "to haul our stuff to town; an' mebbe we can build a new shed to keep ut in."

The Hopper set the catsup bottle on the checks and rubbed his cheek, squinting at the ceiling in the manner of one who means to be careful of his speech.

"They's things wot is an' things wot ain't," he began. "We ain't none o' us ever got nowheres bein' crooked. I been figurin' that I still got about twenty thousan' o' that bunch o' green I pulled out o' that express car, planted in places where 'taint doin' nobody no good. I guess ef I do ut careful I kin send ut back to the company, a little at a time, an' they'd never know where ut come from."

175

A Reversible Santa Claus

Mary wept; Humpy stared, his mouth open, his one eye rolling queerly.

"I guess we kin put a little chunk away every year," The Hopper went on. "We'd be comfortabler doin' ut. We could square up ef we lived long enough, which we don't need t' worry about, that bein' the Lord's business. You an' me's cracked a good many safes, Hump, but we never made no money at ut, takin' out th' time we done."

"He's got religion; that's wot he's got!" moaned Humpy, as though this marked the ultimate tragedy of The Hopper's life.

"Mebbe ut's religion an' mebbe ut's jes' sense," pursued The Hopper, unshaken by Humpy's charge. "They wuz a chaplin in th' Minnesoty pen as used t' say ef we're all square with our own

176

selves ut's goin' to be all right with God.
I guess I got a good deal o' squarin' t' do,
but I'm goin' t' begin ut. An' all these
things happenin' along o' Chris'mus, an'
little Shaver an' his ma bein' so friendly
like, an' her gittin' me t' help straighten
out them ole gents, an' doin' all I done
an' not gettin' pinched seems more 'n jes'
luck; it's providential's wot ut is!"

This, uttered in a challenging tone,
evoked a sob from Humpy, who announced that he "felt like" he was going
to die.

"It's th' Chris'mus time, I reckon,"
said Mary, watching The Hopper deposit
the two checks in the clock. "It's the
only decent Chris'mus I ever knowed!"

THE END

Printed in the United States
135944LV00005B/108/A

9 780548 901786